We, At the End of the World

We, At the End of the World

A collection of new poems by Yang Anda
Translated by Stella Kim

K
POET
아시아

Contents

WE, AT THE END
OF THE WORLD

Invitation

If night and day were humans.

If fire and ash and the forest and the sea... and the
scenes we love

were in fact different aspects of humans.

If night tells day, Let's live on a little more.

I love you. Day responds to night.

If they were twins. But if no one knew which came
first.

I said to you,

Let's live on a little more.

You said to me,

I love you.

A time impossible to tell whether it is dawn or evening.

When waking up from an entangled dream.

If we were twins.

If we had crawled out of the same womb.

Because we can't know the beginning and the end
of the mind.

And if someday a dream of the destruction of the
world begins.

Eternal Night

If the hair on your sleeping head were the darkest strings of a violin. If all the music of the night were colored with darkness.

For some reason, our night is unending. You roll your shoulders, struggling with sleep. I haven't apologized for my insomnia. When we breathe under the covers, your breath echoes into oblivion.

Guessing the lifespan of a lamp and dancing in a dark room. Were we two gazes flying to the darkest place? Because your eyes didn't even miss a glimmer of light. As I found you effortlessly while you danced.

A shadow darker than the darkness passes by the window. The sound of a sudden gust of wind. Listen. That's not the wind. Are you listening? To the sound of machines breathing. An earth-shattering shriek. A colossal mass of shadows.

God and we must be the only ones who love this night. The destruction of the world is irrelevant to us. As we devote ourselves to our love and narrative. Everything is leaning. I might fall while dancing in front of you.

I keep pressing the camera's shutter button. Watching you as you flicker. You vanish. Into the darkness.

You smile. In a flash of light.

Afterworld

When the window trembled, the sound of explosions followed.

"I'm scared," you say, holding my wrist. Now it's impossible to know anything anymore. Afraid I won't wake up if I fall asleep. I don't take a single step out of the room.

The window trembles.

You say, "Laborers were the first." Then you describe how the numerous gears were interlocked and incessantly rotating. "Was it beautiful?"

"It was beautiful.

I saw the capitalists running from the factories."

The window trembles.

The last news said that the students took to the streets with black umbrellas. They demanded what they deserved, but their demand was undeservedly ignored. "The world is silent," said one reporter.

The window trembles.

"After the laborers?"

"Injured children. Then the starving elderly. Then the order became meaningless."

The window trembles.

You bring up your visit to a city.

"When I arrived, everyone was already dead. The streets were blackened with bloody tools and um-brellas. The city was full of ghosts' whispers. There were dead people everywhere, infested with bugs. For no reason I ran through an empty street. Until the tears stopped streaming down my face. Until I could understand sorrow. Waiting for this feeling to stop.

I ran,

as if to make the buildings crumble down.

I ran toward somewhere unknown."

The window trembles.

I see a burning building through the window.

I am a person who stays silent in my room.

A colossal firecracker in my heart.

If We Are Completed in a Painting

The day I saw maggots streaming out of a corpse.

I looked at the canvas you were working on. I couldn't understand your painting for the life of me, but I loved the colors. I felt dizzy to the tips of my toes, meandering through your painting. I stumbled. Your anxiety still remained unbroken.

I wanted to tell you a mysterious story. Ancient buildings, undecaying corpses, and indecipherable cryptograms. A story attempting to comprehend the things that may be forever incomprehensible. But what I wanted to comprehend was, perhaps. . .

Your hair smells of oil. I'm not sure when it started, but whenever I think of you, numerous oil paintings are simultaneously painted and then erased in my head. It would have been great to see the face of the dead with you.

Every night, I dream of being trapped in your canvas. What color rainy season would go with an ashen sky? I close my eyes and recall your scent. Turpentine. That's right, you said it was turpentine. As light bled on the spots touched by raindrops.

Watching the paint drop into a clear water container, without knowing why the image was beautiful, I murmured that it was simply beautiful. That it was beautiful because I did not know why. If convulsing tears are dropped into a water container, how beautiful can that image become?

You forgot about me and ran away into your canvas. Into the snowy white anxiety. Why don't you draw humans, I wondered. And I told you that.

I see the gooseflesh on the nape of your neck. What would it have been like if our blood were different colors. I imagine our skin melting. Dancing maggots.

Hunting Season

The city at night

is pushing away the darkness. To hate it. Insomni-

acs are pulling on the darkness.

To love it.

Outside the window,

the sound of a low-flying airplane.

There's an airport nearby.

That was what I was perceiving

in the city at night.

early every morning,

the sound of a pack of dogs barking

turns this place into a city full of dogs.

Yesterday, I saw dogs bullying a dog. In this city. There are people who have that many dogs. In this city of night.

I wondered,

"Who is the owner of my soul?"

The dogs ran with the alley in their mouths. As though that was their purpose of existence.

Lying on your bed,

I inhale

the smell of medicine, stronger than the scent of

your skin.

Breaking the bottles of pills,

I created ailing music.

To comfort your soul.

Next to their dead owner, the dogs still wag their
tails.

From left to right.

From right to left.

Bouncing back.

Blood and Iron

A child talks about a war fought a hundred years ago.

That the sounds of gunfire continued in the town to that very day. That the soldiers piled the corpses of their comrades on the wheelbarrow. That occasionally when they noticed holes on the back of their dead comrades' heads,

the living wondered,

Who among us?

Another child talks about an ongoing war today.

"When you touch the blood, it smells like a rusty knife.

Foreigners say it smell like gunpowder.

If we make weapons with our blood.

If we kill someone with our blood."

A Glass Rose

Look.

There's the ocean outside the window; the night erases waves; and there is a mirror in this room. But because I can't confirm myself.

Look.

Pacing the room with wallpaper covered in mold. Grains of sand are scattered about. And I can feel the sand under my feet. As the room turns into beach.

You can hear laughter when you trample on dead flowers.

Listen.

It happened in some highlands.

Standing at a grave, Father said,

"Looking after my parents

is my last calling, and

you won't understand me now

but you will come to be like me someday."

A tree and another tree maintain their distance

so they can wave their hands even from afar.

Hoping that thinking that you're lost

will help you see something,

something more beautiful,

finally you

grabbed me by the wrist

and led me to a field of roses.

"People who live here

call these numerous mountains

the mirror mountains. An old story passed down

by word-of-mouth says

that god made a huge mirror that reflects the moun-

tains,

and the mountains and their reflections are both

multiplying in numbers."

Then we kissed.

I asked you about the beauty of night and day.

I asked you about the beauty of fire and ash.

When I looked out through the waterfall,

shards of glass glistened, and they were cold.

I used to think about how close to the reality the

dream is, when I wake up saying,

My wrist is see-through.

What is more beautiful?

Look.

There's the ocean outside the window. It's not trying to hold the waves. Glass is breaking. Glass is breaking. Glass is shattering,

I could have said but didn't. I couldn't believe that I had two ears.

There was always a throng of people. It was a lengthy line, an irregular rhythm and noise, but sounded like a single percussion instrument.

Field of roses.

Field of roses.

Island

At the beach on a colorless night. How can lotuses bloom in the sea? Each lotus with a lit candle in its embrace.

As though the sea is blazing.

Try moving your arms. As you freely moved your arms. Come on, try it. As your arms pushed away the waves.

But I can't get to you at my speed.

I'm scared. What if it gets deep. What if you and I become endlessly deep. I sit on the sandy beach. Watching the blazing colorless sea.

A lotus blooming in the sea. A candlelight blooming on the lotus. Who so loved the flower that they brought it from the lake? So loved the fire.

The sea flares up.

There must have been someone who planted a lotus in the sea. Holding the flower in their hands. Walking to the beach barefoot. Leaving footprints.

I put my foot on the footprint you made. But lotuses don't grow in the sea.

Then that is a story that makes the impossible possible.

Or a story that you made up. As you created the narrative of possibility for me and made a film for the first time.

I can't believe that I'm growing deeper with you.

Afraid to grow deeper. In daunting fear.

When I open my eyes wide.

Because we might find ourselves leaning against each other in a dark hospital room. Because we might be crying, staring at the flickering candlelight.

And the prayer begins.

If we go to the island together.

If we are at the island together.

Because I want to breathe with you for a long time.

You and breath. Because I need both.

Ten Thousand Nights and Days

We decide not to do it again. You are a blood vessel protruding from your arm and a handspan of an ankle, like a joke we'd share in a dream.

Let's go away.

Come away with me.

A dying old man in this place used to be a gardener.

He said that there was a statue of pruning shears symbolizing him in the town he worked all his life.

"Is the forest silence.

They are holding out night and day.

People don't know.

The song of fire and ash.

The image of a forest made up of numerous trees.

Their uproar."

No one doubted his words here. Until the day he mistook a caregiver's finger for a branch in the garden.

When you bleed,

with the ring still on it.

Red flower petals blossom.

Now let's go away.

Go away to that faraway place.

If the tragedy does not end.

I can hear the music. When can we stop the foot-age? Are trees in the future the same as trees in the present?

Gathering nightmares together and throwing them out the door.

Recommending a different door to those looking for a key.

Their tragedy is theirs. Reading the pages of our

tragedy.

I was born with the dream of a snake. There was a dream and a name that came before me. Someone said that I was wearing the snakeskin and spoke,

another said I bit their wrist.

Is the ocean dynamic?

Not knowing by whose intention the same waves repeat. In the heart

both the forest and the sea coexist. They do not stop the repetition. It is getting swept to the beach after getting lost and lost again in some forest.

Always lacking sunlight. Always excessive shades.

Revolving blood. Waves.

Dizzying.

It's dizzying.

Unnecessary slumber.

Because blood may spill from all the pores of our
body

if we say we are not hurt.

But we decide not to part again. This being the last
time.

As if we have loved again.

As if we are dying again.

I had something to say to anyone before leaving.

The person fighting with the forest, a corpse under

the cliffs. Or an animal in slumber.

Now is the time to run to anywhere.

The second hand is moving.

They were cutting.

Our hearts were. Our sorrows were.

With the Map of the Night Spread Open

Then, we bought one-way tickets. In the plaza, people holding flags were throwing firebombs and chanting slogans. We won't live for long. When we were about to step away, someone threw themselves off the spire.

The blazing forest is repetitively beautiful but dizzying. Ashes were scattering in the wind, and you said it was a black snowstorm. If you look at the sea, we are submerged half in fire, half in water. Our faces are distorting.

We picked flowers for the dead animals. Putting

two flower petals over the eyes. Learning to put our hands together even though we don't believe in gods. If there is an afterworld, it would be great to be buried in flowers there. Hoping that the fire path they experienced would be a field of flowers in their dream.

The night bus rattles as though a tire might come off at any time. Crumpled into the back seat, I watched. You, leaning against my shoulder and sleeping. A faint light shining in through the windows settling on your face. I gathered and wrote down things you said in your sleep. If this becomes our last will.

I like ailing windows. Because I can blow on them and draw anything. Drawing a readily erased dream. You know, we didn't want the name of a fate that would disappear, so why do we keep on limping?

Dream's Joke

"I had a nightmare." As tears roll down your face. "Someone was coming at me with a knife in their back pocket." I pull you into my embrace. "He cut my ears and gouged out my eyes." As I touch your eyes.

Your ankles are white and cold. When I think of fire, I think of light, not darkness. When the cold wind blows in through the double pane window. "I'll tell you about the dream," you said. You stood at a podium and read the names of the dead written on the slate. The last one was yours.

"Now it's your turn." You want more dreams. Asking me to tell you irrepressibly explosive narratives. I think of a forest that grows past the timberline. As I tell you about the love of the forest. Without telling you that it's a lie.

Let me tell you about my dream. People whose jobs are to hurt people were wading through a wet fog. While the wet fog became tinged scarlet with blood, lovers made last confessions of their love. We hide in each other's blood. As your ankles turn to red, hot fire.

But one day when we are submerged in a wet fog.

You'll face the images of the dream in real life. And I won't be able to hear your voice anymore. Unable to close my mouth. I won't be able to see you and I won't be able to shed tears. I hold you and comfort you. I cover your ears with my hands. And your eyes. And checking the color of your ankles.

We, At the End of the World

When we were heading there. Walking on an unending snow path. To find some light. I thought. We need a house. A parachute and a song titled "Airbag" or "Fence" and a rope to tie around my ankle. I believed that falling into someone's heart was love. Following the footprints you left, I heard the snow scream. We walked until we turned white. To a place where you could breathe or hide. Growing smaller into a dot toward the horizon. It is infinite. The horizon recedes and becomes unreachable. We leave an infinite number of footprints and the snowstorm erases our footprints, you see. Thinking that your breath is like a song from some snowy country. Let me tell you a story. About before I met you. When I was a teenier tinier soul than now. A thought that my heart had been simply transparent then. When I touched the water it became immersed in blue, and it became colorful when I walked through a field of flowers. Now my heart is blood red, even if you cut it and closely examine it. Why is the dream from then different from the dream from now. What is making us this way. Are you listening? When we get there. Even if there is no house, no parachute, no song titled Airbag or Fence, and no rope to tie around my ankle. Indescribable emptiness. Or the biggest fire in the world. A fistful of snow we ate to quench our thirst. Let me tell you another story. Are you listening? It's too early to go to sleep. You smiled. Your eyes turning into long crescent moons. I shook your shoulders. You have to listen to my story. Don't close your eyes.

Rainy Season

To remember the past, those were days when it rained in a small room. I made paper boats out of all the pieces of paper that listed the history of your illness. Hoping it would float away. Like us now. Like time did then.

It was midday when climate darker than dawn continued. We cut the damaged ends of each other's hair and became neat and tidy. When we kept the door open a handspan, the damp breeze that flew from somewhere far vibrated between us.

Because we believed that all sick things can sparkle. Sticking neon stars on tears in wallpaper. We dream of things like snow melting at a dangerous speed, a flash of sunlight between pieces of dark cloud, and the sky reflected in a puddle.

But I don't know which beach you are thinking of as you groan under illness. I don't know in which climate it is shining. Just as you don't know what I'm thinking as I look at you.

Even when my heart was rolling around in a ditch, you walked on my right. Penny for your thoughts, you said. I thought about last night's dream, I answered. How was the weather there? You asked.

In the days without light or hope. But in the days knowing that there is light behind the clouds. Even though we laughed a little and cried a lot.

Massaging your convulsing arms and legs every time you fall asleep. Thinking about it now, did our stifled cries become the music of the night. Or perhaps the sound of raindrops outside the window. In some dream, we lie on the beach, listening to the waves.

On some nights, I crumbled helplessly but didn't build myself up again. Singing of your convulsing sleep again. Grains of sand glistening on the beach. I saw your tears twinkle in the dark.

But the paper boats never sailed. Stuck at our feet, the paper boats sank but your illness never lightened. Washing your body, you hide your tears under the water. While our room keeps on getting wet and immersed and the wallpaper keeps on tearing.

You don't know how many oceans I crossed to come here to you from my last dream. You don't know that I crumble every time we hold hands. Waves crushing against a sandy beach. As my fingers cover the back of your hand.

Blackout

I want to be a bird in my next life, you said. When I become a bird, I'll only perch on the tallest trees. So that you can find me when you come to a swaying tree. In the distance I saw children walking on a path in the woods. Suddenly I thought some heavy rain would be nice. But you spoke. You have to be fire. Be fire and burn down all the tallest trees. So that I can never find you. We decided to do that. In my dream, I was burning up. I saw a bird flying into the fire.

To Death Ostracized by Angels

There is someone who plants flower trees on the beach.

And I woke from a dream where you die in the future.

The audience who watched my dream left the theater.

You were holding a bouquet of flowers in your arms.

*

Sometime in the past when the late summer heat began. We went to the town where I was born.

You said there was something we needed to see in

this place.

There is a fascinating legend about this lake.

We wanted to promise eternal love by walking around the lake three times, but the lake was endless.

Ripples that spread from the throw of a stone.

We understood the shape of the ripples as the heart of the lake.

That izakaya there, wasn't it nice?

The owner was kind too. Though we were intimated by his hooked nose and busy eyebrows.

He was a person who gave out bite-sized potato chips and finger food to the homeless.

With unexpected kindness, he took care to give us bedding.

How did the cookie taste?

It's our town's specialty. Baked with ingredients grown on our land.

We purchased all the cookies from the famous shops in five alleys. We chewed with our molars all night.

The sound of crumpling paper bags.

*

This was a dream that begins in some hospital room.

Through a machine, I could see

whether your old heart was still beating.

Your forehead was cold.

I massaged your arms and legs,

pulled up the comforter to your chin,

and on your forehead

I placed my hand.

That was the first time I touched your forehead.

The day I slipped out of the hospital room,

the children were playing with a dead bird.

Like playing catch one day.

I blankly stared at them

tossing and catching the dead bird with red hands.

There was a fedora on the roof of the hospital.

A pair of lips opened under the fedora.

"Even that little bird has a heart."

A child asked me,

"Angels are real, right?"

"Yes. You were one once."

*

"There's something we have to see," you said.

Two sets of black clothes.

A white flower, a blue flower.

Two types of fruits.

Oh, right. We need alcohol too.

Out of the city into the suburbs.

Growing farther away.

A cemetery in the sky.

No need to rush. I'll wait here. The cab driver brought

a cigarette to his lips.

And we, to one of the numerous graves.

*

This is a dream that begins by a grave.

When the old you asked me who was buried in
this grave,

I answered that it was the grave of a revolutionary.

You asked me what a revolutionary was. It seemed
that you'd forgotten the meaning of "revolutionary."

Not knowing how to explain it,

I ended up evading an answer.

"This is the grave of a king."

"The grave of a king," said the old you.

"That's right. A king is buried here."

Then

As if you were seeing something like this for the first time.

Staggering as though you didn't care if you went blind.

Under the pouring summer sunlight.

You kept on muttering.

This is the grave of a king...

A king is buried under here...

*

A stream of visitors came to the funeral home even until early morning. You were smiling brightly in the memorial photo, but people were shedding tears.

Numerous flowers on the shrine.

"Do we go to a field of flowers when we die?"

"That's right. We were born covered in a red petal."

*

The day late summer heat rolled on.

With fruits and alcohol at the grave

You, more diseased than the grave, placed flowers in a vase. In a rusty cab, we drove out of the cemetery in the sky. And I dreamed that you died in the future.

The audience for my next dream was entering the theater.

And I was holding your ashes in my embrace.

Small Theater

The last scene on that day ended with someone pulling a trigger.

Then a blackout.

Numerous journals in the drawer. Numerous mes in the journals. As I rewind myself.

Hello.

Child who covers up lies with lies.

Who strikes the wall with his fist in a fit of anger.

Black blood. Black night. Black heart.

Child

who believes that the meaner he become the cooler

he gets.

On a rainy day, the child got on a bicycle

Abandoned on a street and pedaled. To get away.

But from what. Grasping a broken brake.

He bawled in the pouring rain.

As the bicycle moved the tears and the rain moved

the crying.

Heavily. More heavily. As the bicycle rolled on

To an unknown place.

The second hand keeps on moving

Even if you don't check that it's moving with your

own eyes. Sad. I cried because that made me sad.

Because it floated away. The bicycle was moving. And I kept on being swept up.

I was sad. That I was changing.

Because the direction was downward.

"I'm sorry."

I comforted a friend at the funeral. Although I hadn't killed his mother.

I'm sorry.

Although I didn't know why I was sorry.

Hoping that my friend would stop crying

If I was sorry.

Early in the morning. A drunkard sleeping on the street.

My friend and I pretended to help him up. While checking his pockets.

When we found a bloody kitchen knife deep inside his coat.

What do we do?

What do we do with this?

Our eyes met and we shivered in cold.

And

we slashed our wrists together.

"We're friends, right?"

There were a few children on the school grounds

at night.

"If we're friends, you'll do this for me, right?"

As the children nodded.

We gathered big stones in the flowerbed and

Threw them at the window. As though we'd made

a resolution.

To be meaner and meaner.

Fireworks start going off.

In our ungrowing hearts.

In our growing sorrow.

Because there was nothing to destroy in the tiny studio apartment. We shared a cigarette. Emptying and breaking bottles.

We destroyed ourselves. Blood staining the broken pieces.

We cut each other's bodies.

Smiling together.

We'll have to stop at some point.

Without looking back.

Since we have to go far when it's time. Kicking at the wing mirror. Saying we won't look back then.

But if our fireworks no longer go off.

The first image of that day begins with someone's
sobbing voice.

And lights.

Bye. Child whose heart is over.

Child

who has become meaner than ever could be.

The world continues to revolve

Even if I don't die myself. I know. Because I know
so well.

Greater sorrow. Smaller heart.

On the stage called the world, an actor playing a

.

god enters. Without a referee. Without forgiveness.

Watching the audience.

I wanted to see myself on the screen, on the screen,
on the screen.

Gross. The blue veins on the back of my hand.

Behind the Scenes

The night passes. With two severed feet. If some-one hid their murderous intentions through this.

When looking to summer for the reason for light-ing a firecracker.

We were standing in an empty lot. Rubbing the blood trickling down from our ears. This was the end. Grasping a two-by-four with the other hand.

There was no boy who called himself a boy. What are you thinking? What are you thinking? Watching your expression swell up as you hold your breath.

I wonder what is in the hand you hid behind your back.

The animal that has failed at hunting again today

is limping. The night passes. With four severed feet.

While someone wasn't able to hide their sorrow with this darkness. I was trying hard to erase my expression.

As the applause showers the stage.

Fire and Ash

Were the too many dances a problem?

Were the songs I sang every night okay?

What about listening to the birds chirping through an open window?

I don't know. And the one who doesn't know is sad.

When you woke after a good dream, you drew it and

When you woke after a nightmare, you looked for me.

What would have it been like had there been a couple of lovers who were our opposites somewhere in this world. Often I dream of being you and falling ill.

Sad. Sad. No matter how many times I say it, the word is not sad enough, so

I thought about a huge sadness I've never had. To give it your name.

In the dream, I stared at a man who split logs endlessly.

The man said his goal was to

cut down the whole forest and ultimately his arm.

Would he be able to reach his goal?

I don't know. And the one who doesn't know is sad.

The mirror mountains. That is where I am now.

We were, very beautiful then.

There, I will finish the picture you couldn't finish.

Fell ill and died, fell ill, or will be falling ill... But I also don't draw people.

A few days ago, I received the news of a death. I smiled a little. Because I thought about the line between significant death and insignificant death now that you aren't here.

Big sadness and small sadness.

We used to play a childish game about whose love was greater.

And it always ended with us both claiming that we won. Only now I admit that I lost. I just lost.

How did I lose?

I don't know. And the one who doesn't know is sad.

Death begins now.

I can finally see my destination. The place where the sick or the will-be sick will turn to fire and ash.

It is all because of you. Of course, I'm kidding.

You used to be greatly surprised by even the smallest jokes. You were someone who

used to startle and fall at the small disturbances and cried, hugging yourself, at the smallest sadness.

Every night, I dream of being trapped in your canvas.

I listen to the song of fire and ash.

I watch the forest's commotion.

The window trembles.

The window trembles.

Is the firecracker going off?

This world is the same.

Maybe I need protection.

Eternal Light

When I pull the curtains and the light pours in.
And if the dead you were sleeping on the bed.

White light and morning and it is the beginning of
the day.

If something with the texture of sunlight pours in.
I think I need to sleep a little longer. You rub your
sleepy eyes.

The world behind the curtains is unfamiliar and
you are sleeping in front of me. Where is this place?
I feel suffocated.

Not knowing how light is created.

I stroked your sleeping corner. I couldn't believe it at all.

Curtain Call

I decide to love crying.

See you later,

if we wave our hands

and show each other the back of our heads,

If tears are the jewels of face.

If flower beds wither in heaps with every step.

When a bird breaks away from the flock.

If you can't understand the difference

between see you later and farewell.

I fail in the scene where I shouldn't look back.

But if we do not call each other.

POET'S NOTES

When writing poetry,

there is a question that people always ask.

What do you think poetry is?

I don't think much about it.

I don't want to think of poetry as something sacred,

but I also don't want to consider it nothing.

So I answer, Poetry is like a game.

A game that I can play by myself.

With no one paying attention to me.

A game like that. I said that many times.

One day, someone asked me the same question.

What do you think poetry is?

And added, People today think poetry is useless.

For some reason I thought for a long time before giving an answer.

Perhaps I was rather depressed that day.

Or perhaps I didn't want to accept that poetry was useless.

I'm not sure. But after a little while,

I answered, "A dance you dance alone."

A dance you dance alone.

But every time I danced,

I was always with someone.

POET'S ESSAY

If we can be eternal at the end of the world

A long time ago, when we first met, he said to me,

"I think we'll make good friends. What do you think?"

Sure, I answered, out of courtesy.

But now, we have become good friends.

He and I are very different kinds of people. Not that you can't grow close to someone you're different from. But we are two extremes. If there was a soul that was the polar opposite of me, I thought it would be him.

He made the following list of our differences:

1. His staple food is salad.

2. He's not much of a drinker.

3. He likes taking strolls.

4. He has mood swings.

5. He's in poor health.

6. He doesn't like literature.

7. He doesn't like films(he really dislikes grotesque scenes. Particularly, in horror films).

8. He likes Disney animations.

9. He likes desserts.

10. He's self-centered.

After mulling over the list, I asked, "What does number 5 have to do with being friends? And I don't think number 10 is completely true."

"No, that's the decisive one."

I couldn't accept his view, so I came up with my own list as follows:

1. My staple is instant foods.

2. I enjoy drinking.

3. I like to lie around.

4. I don't really have mood swings.

5. I'm in good health (He raised an objection to this.)

6. I like literature.

7. I like films.

8. I don't like Disney animations.

9. I don't like desserts.

10. I'm not altruistic.

"What do you think?" I asked, and he said, "I'm not convinced."

The reason I thought we couldn't be friends was not because we were different people. It's because I tend to keep a certain distance from someone I meet for the first time.

But we grew close rather quickly, sometimes spending days together. I remember being with him on August 9, 2019, as well.

"Today's my 10,000th day on earth."

"How did you know that? People count that?"

I couldn't remember how I knew.

After he wakes up, he makes sketches in his notebook. When he has a good dream. But on many of the nights we spent together, he woke up crying or I woke up to find him in tears. I asked him why, and every time he said, No reason.

No reason.

I no longer ask him why and just comfort him.

According to the list of our 10 differences that I can't accept, he's not in good health. He often talks as if he's already dead. That makes me sad.

Occasionally he talks as if this world has already been destroyed. I thought he was making a leap of logic at first, but these days they sound like metaphors.

The world that he talks of is probably his world. Possibly one that I'm a part of.

While spending time with him, I didn't eat any instant foods, drank less, and walked down a lot of streets. I spent less time lying around and started experiencing what I couldn't see before. Now I relish eating salads.

When I experience something new, I think of at least two new ideas.

"Want to read a new poem I wrote?" He tells me he doesn't really get poetry but answers, "Sure," and reads it.

He was the first to read all the poems in this collection. He didn't say whether a poem was good or bad. Instead, he told me his impressions, It's depressing. It's sad. Or it's interesting.

And his impressions were helpful.

He likes listening to me telling him about movies. Movies in genres he can't bring himself to watch. I have difficulty explaining what I felt when watching them.

He enjoys listening to my worries. My worries about poetry. Most of the time, he simply listens. Occasionally he answers in his own way.

And his answers were helpful.

Except for a few, I haven't published or shown most of the poems in this book to other people. If anyone asks me why, I think I'll say,

Just because.

I just thought that I should keep them that way.

I like the phrase "no reason." Often times, you have a clear-cut reason for hating something, but not necessarily for liking something. So those times, I answer, No reason, and I feel better.

Every time I feel unclear about something, I realize anew that I'm alive. I write because I know how to move my hand, I eat because I know how to move my arm, I dance because I know how to move my feet, and I'm alive because my heart is beating. But the thought that I'm not just a sum of all these things. And the mystery that I'm alive for some unclear reason begins. He probably won't be able to stay my friend forever. And when that happens, I might walk the streets by myself, experience something new, watch Disney animations, and eat salad by myself. And perhaps I'll come to enjoy desserts by then.

He tells me that I'm an altruistic person. I tell him that I do it for selfish reasons. I act considerately because it makes me feel better. I do it for my own ease of mind. So I'm the most selfish person in the world.

If someone in the distant universe looks into humans with a microscope, everyone will look sick. I'm also sick. He's in worse condition than I am, but he healed me.

He's the most altruistic person I know. Sometimes unnecessarily. And I told him so.

He doesn't believe me. I wrote this long piece but what I really want is

to tell him, thank you,

for no (specific) reason.

Actually, I've already told him. Many times.

I'd like to read this book aloud with him.

And I hope that his world stays intact for a long time. Possibly one that I'm a part of.

COMMENTARY

Mirrors and Mise-en-Scène

Shin Su-jin (Literary critic)

1. World, end, us

We, at the end of the world. The title is rather ambitious, almost heroic. The facts that there has been a series of poetry collections using the word "world" in the title to mean a general and ultimate inclusiveness, that the "end" was established as an albeit tragic and futile virtuality, and that an ultimate sense of identity that combines you and I—"we"—appears in the poems all point to an all-too familiar trend, but at the same time, they reveal Yang Anda's unique sentiments.

The poems feature a first person narrator—"I." What encroaches every corner of the narrator's world is "you," who forms an inseparable pair with the narrator like twins—or night and day. In Yang's poetry, only "you" and "me" remain in this world. The narrator is closer to an adolescent in that he does not have a stable living situation, balanced thinking, forward-looking planning, or productive interactions with others. This extreme proposition, in which only love is equated to the entire world, becomes the prerequisite to understanding Yang's poetry.

The reality of the world reminiscent of a dystopia continues to repeat like a nightmare for the narrator. However, there is no consideration for the probability or the structural understanding of how the world came to be in such tragedy. Only the narrator plainly discloses that "the destruction of the world is irrelevant to us"("Eternal Night"). Like Deleuze's uneven paving stones, the misery of the world only seems to be a necessity to display the main characters' pure love. Although the poems describe situations reminiscent of war, famine, and other disasters, they are never specified or foregrounded. And as a result they are closer to artificial images, like the stories in video games.

Yang's poems, created with the three elements— the world, end, and us—show signs of becoming a grand narrative, but they do not feature any serious problems or lead to specific incidents. The narrator "I" is helpless and neither fights or reconciles with the world, and his coordinates in time and history are completely nonexistent, revealing only his exaggerated sensibilities and monologues. In a situation where nothing happens despite the destruction of the world, only the endless proliferation of simulacra fill up the poet's small room.

This structure in which society is intentionally omitted to lay bare the narrator's sense of identity is a fictional contraption that covers the whole world with impossibilities under the themes of isolation, crisis, and love. And this structure is continuously produced in series. Then let us take a look at the mechanism in which Yang's impossibilities, which pass through the world, end, and us, are invented.

2. An invitation to the night: the display of fear as an indecipherable foreign film

This poetry collection begins with "Invitation" and ends with "Curtain Call." "Invitation" is a poem that serves as a rite of passage into Yang Anda's world and, therefore, features various signs that help us read the poet's mind. The first is the poet's humanization, or emotionalization, where he sees everything, even day and night, as humans.

Like day and night, which no one can tell "which came first," and a "time impossible to tell whether" it is dawn or evening, an "entangled dream" and reality, and a mind whose "beginning and the end" cannot be found, the narrator and "you" cannot be distinguished. The narrator "I" can't objectively see himself, and as a result "I" becomes "you" and vice versa. It is impossible to know whether the dream of the world's destruction begins because of "you" or because of the narrator, who is forever unable to know "you." The only thing we know is that "you" is the entire world, and "I" has become "you"—and everything is falling out of its place.

"When the window trembled, the sound of explosions followed.

'I'm scared,' you say, holding my wrist. Now it's impossible to know anything anymore. Afraid I won't wake up if I fall asleep.

I don't take a single step out of the room.

The window trembles.

You say, "Laborers were the first." Then you describe how the numerous gears were interlocked and incessantly rotating. "Was it beautiful?"

"It was beautiful."

-Excerpt from "Afterworld"

The chilling realization that there we do not know anything turns into a series of fear. When "you" say "I'm scared," holding "my" wrist, the reason for "your" fear is not the sound of explosions that make the window tremble. The fear arises from the existential terror of "you," "I," and the world as objects that cannot be recognized. That is why we do not know the time and location of this war-like situation, which unfolds like a foreign movie to show the truth about the narrator who has become incapable of perceiving what is happening around him.

"You" confess that "laborers were the first," that the scene in which "numerous gears were interlocked and incessantly rotating" was beautiful, and that you saw "the capitalists running from the factories." Then the mention of "injured children" and the "starving elderly," and how the order became meaningless afterward reflect the narrator's guilt, as do the reporter's words: "The world is silent."

The city where bloodied tools and umbrellas cover the streets of death infested with bugs may be a fictional image that came from Charlie Chaplin's "Modern Times" or Franz Kafka's "Metamorphosis", but it serves as evidence of narrator's sense of injustice and uncomfortable truth. Only the daunting fear of a long and steep staircase called economic inequality and the boundary between aboveground and underground are becoming clear, while the boundary between what is human and inhuman is blurring. In all this, how should a human being survive?

But in this apocalyptic painting of hell, Yang reduces the feelings of fear, guilt, sorrow, chaos, and anxiety that arise from the injustices and inability to perceive in two short phrases: "I am a person who stays silent in my room. A colossal firecracker in my heart." Despite the rampant death around him, the narrator repeatedly mentions that the window trembled and ruminates on its beauty. This attitude toward the pessimistic reality creates a sense of discordance.

The poet consistently maintains the belief that the world is doomed. One child talks about a war from 100 years ago while another child talks about today's war. It became impossible to tell "who among us" killed the people who have died under endless gunfire("Blood and Iron"), and while living our blood smelled of "rusty knife" and "gunpowder." This place, which allegorically shows the chain of evil, similar to the original sin, through the relationship between blood and iron, is not at all a just or true world but a place where terrible violence, lies, and death are perpetrated.

3. The frame of internalization and the transformation of existence

It is irrelevant whether this world in ruins exists in the middle ages or today or the future, or any other time period. It is because this is a typical backdrop set in virtual reality. This situation, in which only "you" and "I" remain after the end of the world, contributes to the narrator's absolutization of "you."

"The day I saw maggots streaming out of a corpse.

[…]

Every night, I dream of being trapped in your canvas. What color rainy season would go with an ashen sky? I close my eyes and recall your scent. Turpen-

tine. That's right, you said it was turpentine. As light
bled on the spots created by raindrops.

Watching the paint drop into a clear water container, without knowing why the image was beautiful, I
murmured that it was simply beautiful. That it was
beautiful because I did not know why. If convulsing
tears are dropped into a water container, how beautiful can that image become?

You forgot about me and ran away into your canvas. Into the snowy white anxiety. Why don't you
draw humans, I wondered. And I told you that.
    -Excerpt from "If We Are Completed in a Painting"

The narrator's derealistic actions, in which he
stays cooped up in his room despite the explosions
and revolution taking place outside his window, is
a result from the sense that the narrator is observ-

ing himself from outside of his body. The gaze of this split identity that appears in verses such as "If we are completed in a painting" or "every night, I dream of being trapped in your canvas" hints at a metacomposition, where the narrator observes himself within a frame.

The narrator "I" feels that paint drops on the painting are beautiful because they are abstract. Just as he wonders whether the chaos have reached a point of beauty without a care for the destruction of the outside world, the narrator thinks that "your" painting is beautiful because he cannot understand it. Beauty reaches a peak in the dramatic moment in which "you" hides in the absolute exclusion, "[forgetting] about me and [running] into your canvas," "into the snowy white anxiety," where "you" don't "draw humans." The fear of the unknown is reflected in the mirror and also refracted into beauty.

In the painting, the narrator is transformed into a

virtual image, which is mainly explained by "maggots streaming out of a corpse." This is a method of transforming a character to jump to a different world of fantasy—dreams. That is why "night," which is the backdrop for most of the poems, becomes the object of equivocal feelings, both hated and loved ("Hunting Season").

"Look.

There's the ocean outside the window; the night erases waves; and there is a mirror in this room. But because I can't confirm myself.

[…]

'People who live here

call these numerous mountains

the mirror mountains. An old story passed down by word-of-mouth says

that god made a huge mirror that reflects the mountains,

and the mountains and their reflections are both increasing in number.'"

-Excerpt from "A Glass Rose"

The room that the narrator is like a vacuum—it is impossible to tell time or space. There is a mirror there, but the narrator "can't confirm [himself]." He cannot see his reflection in the mirror. And even if he can, he cannot tell whether the reflection is himself or someone else. The room he is in continues to transform into a beach with "wallpaper covered in mold," "dead flowers," and "sand under [his] feet." And he says that his surrounding is more beautiful because he is lost, because there are things that only those who are lost can see.

The motif of mirror (like the mountains reflected in a god's mirror keeps on multiplying) leads to inexplicable dreams, and upon waking up the narrator swings in and out of dream and reality like a pendulum.

To the narrator, a nightmare consists of mysterious senses, such as a "throng of people" and "a lengthy line," "irregular rhythm," and "noise" that come together as a "single percussion instrument." This is a fantasy that is only permitted in the night, and it is the pathos that the poet fears yet continues to seek. Ultimately what Yang Anda is searching for by creating countless frames is the mise-en-scène of a beautiful yet mysterious story that can be summed up in three words: beginning, unfamiliarity, and possibility.

4. The race of simulacra that ends in a dark hospital room

The struggle that appears in many of Yang's poems is described by a series of images—plaza, flags, firebombs, slogans, spire, jumping off buildings to death, and signs of suicide ("With the Map of the Night

Spread Open"). However, as per Baudrillard's famous statement, images that reflect reality become irrelevant to reality by hiding the reality and even the lack of reality. The disintegration of the world that frequently raises its head in Yang's poems is not a reproduction of reality. Instead, the chaotic nights of the narrator, who acquired a unique inner self through an encounter with the images of an apocalyptic world, resonate with a song as they wander through a "blazing forest."

Discarded from a network or a system both voluntarily and involuntarily, the narrator follows death, unable to withstand anxiety, solitude, and sorrow any longer. Unlike the concepts of inequality, isolation, and brutal violence, the images of night are assembled into a forest, beach, corpses, fire, and ashes. And these images make up the narrator's own world, which functions regardless of reality, and become absolute sanctums.

The narrator hovers between light and darkness, dream and reality, memory and oblivion, and life and death. Yet despite the precarious condition he is in and the vertigo he feels, his clock is set to the night. The twenty five poems in this collection store the voice of the narrator who takes the last stand to protect his world in symbolic objects and repeat it as an endless nightmare. If a dream continues for the narrator, who lives in the dream, then the dream is no longer a dream but reality.

Gathering nightmares together and throwing them out the door.

Recommending a different door to those looking for a key.

Their tragedy is theirs. Reading the pages of our tragedy.

-Excerpt from "Ten Thousand Nights and Days"

I can't believe that I'm becoming deeper with you. Afraid to be deeper. In daunting fear.

When I opened my eyes wide.

Because we might find ourselves leaning against each other in a dark hospital room. Because we might be crying, staring at the flickering candlelight.

-Excerpt from "Island"

At the end of the world, with a hunch that "now is the time to run to anywhere," the narrator repeats the need for him and "you" to leave. To the people "looking for a key," the narrator recommends a door that can be opened with a key and states, "Their tragedy is theirs." But he himself does not look for a key and instead stands in front of a door that cannot be opened with a key. And now he has to read a page from his own tragedy. "Getting swept to the beach after getting lost and lost again in some forest" is a kind of divine punishment, but the narrator does not try to hide his pride and vanity he has about his wanderings.

Poetry is essentially an admiration of something that is impossible in reality; it is not something you can experience or be aware of. With "you," the narrator grows deeper and deeper into the depths of fiction and the unconscious. It is similar to perverted self-regression. Ultimately, the self-sufficient fantasy of a "made up story," the "narrative of possibility", and the "film [made] for the first time" cannot but arrive at a dark hospital room.

5. The death of "you" met at the end of a journey with a limp

In the poems based on a vicious narrative of growth, full of lies, tricks, violence, delinquency, and sense of shame, there is "no boy who call[s] himself a boy" ("Behind the Scenes"). But the scene soon changes to one where the narrator says, "I need pro-tection" ("Fire and Ash"). The limping boy is the face of darkness behind the scenes. The "limp" that appears in several poems shows that the narrator is looking straight at his own gait.

The narrator thinks that the blue veins on the back of his hand is "gross" ("Small Theater"). This represents his current condition, in which he cannot objec-tively accept his existing self. Instead, the narrator sees his own destruction as the destruction of the world and concentrates on writing a narrative that does not follow logic or reason. And he persistently observes his past self, stuck in a frame.

Why is the dream from then different from the dream from now. What is making us this way. Are you listening? When we get there. Even if there is no house, no parachute, no song titled Airbag or Fence, and no rope to tie around my ankle. Indescribable emptiness. Or the biggest fire in the world. A fistful of snow we ate to quench our thirst. Let me tell you another story. Are you listening? It's too early to go to sleep. You smiled. Your eyes turning into long crescent moons. I shook your shoulders. You have to listen to my story. Don't close your eyes.

-Excerpt from "We, at the End of the World"

The place where the two people "walking on an unending snow path" is not a place of everyday life where they have house chores to do or bills to pay. It is not a place where even a magnetic field of social issues and networks can reach. Everything is still and unmoving in this place, like in a vacuum. Only the night and day come to this place of stories and pill bottles.

It is clear that the characters in the poems are dreaming of a home, symbolic of stability, protection, and solidarity. Even though the narrator wants to tell "you" a story, asking if "you" is listening, and even though he is anxious, shaking "your" shoulders and telling "you" it's too early to sleep, "you" end up closing "your" eyes. The conversation between "you, who is not here" and "I, who remembers" is the idea that remains consistent throughout this poetry collection.

God and we must be the only ones who love this night. The destruction of the world is irrelevant to us. As we devote ourselves to our love and narrative. Everything is tilting. I might fall while dancing in front of you.

I keep pressing the camera's shutter button. Watching you as you flicker. You vanish. Into the darkness. You smile. In a flash of light.

-Excerpt from "Eternal Night"

The narrator tells "you" the story of the love of a forest that grows past the timberline, "without telling 'you' that it's a lie" ("Dream's Joke"). This act of writing poems about the stories that the narrator is dreaming of creates an effect of a picture frame. The dreams in the dream are magical and romantic.

In the dreams, "you" flicker and fade away. Despite the narrator's desire to keep "you" for even just a fleeting moment, "you" are gone. In "Eternal Light," which feels like a twin poem of "Eternal Night," the narrator sees "you" sleeping under the pouring light. But even "you" who appears to be either dead or sick to the narrator cannot provide a complete salvation.

This scene seems like an ending, in which "you" who was everything to the narrator dies like an angel, but it actually signals the beginning. It is because this scene is not a representation of the narrator's repeating nightmares or the fantasies he creates but the narrator's very first experience with real light that pierces into his darkness. The moment the outside light encounters the darkness inside, "you"—who is in fact the narrator within himself—is able to shed the shell of the narrator's deformed twin and become the other.

6. Curtain call

In a life where "flower beds wither in heaps with every step," the narrator decides to "love crying." It is because he is a poet—one who willingly embraces all deterioration. That is why he "fails in the scene where [he] shouldn't look back." He is someone who is determined to look back—a poor man who cannot but eat away at himself even if all he has are vulgar and contemptible memories. This poem is how the poet defines himself; it is the poetics of his confession.

There was a time when the essence of literature lay in the self that was discordant with the world. There once was a beautiful scene where a lumpen intellectual indulged in degenerative entertainment sat gathering sunlight through a magnifying glass. As he wrote word after word of his own misery to compose "Crow's-eye View," his limping manuscript dreamed of wings.

Now, within the frame of mirrors and mise-en-scène, Yang Anda continues to create nightmares of the night and labyrinths in the woods, carving the traces of "me" who walks with a limp and "you" who falls into a languid slumber. He engraves "your" absence and "my" loss in front of the world represented by "you," who is fading in the inevitable and irreversible. Yet all the while, rejecting everything.

WHAT
THEY SAY
ABOUT
YANG ANDA

POET

The future is a scenery that has not yet arrived—
it is the gateway to boundless imagination. Yet the
poet attempts to put it in a "small book of the future" and turn it into a small secret as a gift for the
present. We are too familiar with the construction
of the antinomic imagination of attempting to mold
the boundless future in graspable language, the
search for an escape from the present, and the desire to seize the present once again. Like the many
names it has—dream, soul, or utopia—it is the di-
vulgence of the beautiful future we seek.

Park Dong-eok, *Book of a Small Future*,
Hyundae Munhak, 2018

Although it seems like a cliched trope of a new
world behind the mirror, Yang Anda's mirror is different. It doesn't help one escape from his world nor
is it connected to a different world. Not only that,
this mirror can't even let one thoroughly examine
himself. These aspects of the mirror plainly explain

Yang's worldview. Yang doesn't attempt to define the world; he simply observes and asks questions. When such action takes place in front of a screen called the mirror, the self collides with the world. As it becomes impossible for one to tell whether the observer is someone else looking in from outside the screen or himself looking at his own self inside the screen, the two beings—one inside the screen and the one outside—gradually overlap. If the being outside the screen is a god of the world outside, Yang becomes a god of the world inside. From a far, Yang seems uncertain, deferring all decisions; but upon a closer look you can see that he is actively looking for himself rather than staying passively locked inside the screen. When you think about it, the breath that started all the questions was, in fact, his own. This is the way Yang lives in this world.

Choe Baek-gyu, "Since when did we become us?:
The World of Yang Anda," Hyundae Munhak, 2018

K-Poet
We, At the End of the World

Written by Yang Anda | **Translated by** Stella Kim
Published by ASIA Publishers | 445, Hoedong-gil, Paju-si, Gyeonggi-do, Korea
(Seoul Office: 161-1, Seodal-ro, Dongjak-gu, Seoul, Korea)
Homepage Address www.bookasia.org | **Tel** (822).821.5055 | **Fax** (822).821.5057
ISBN 979-11-5662-317-5 (set) | 979-11-5662-449-3 (04810)
First published in Korea by ASIA Publishers 2020

This book is published with the support of the Literature Translation Institute of Korea
(LTI Korea).

K-픽션 한국 젊은 소설

최근에 발표된 단편소설 중 가장 우수하고 흥미로운 작품을 엄선하여 출간하는 〈K-픽션〉은 한국문학의 생생한 현장을 국내외 독자들과 실시간으로 공유하고자 기획되었습니다. 원작의 재미와 품격을 최대한 살린 〈K-픽션〉 시리즈는 매 계절마다 새로운 작품을 선보입니다.

Through literature, you
bilingual Edition Modern

ASIA Publishers' carefully selected

Set 1		Set 2	

Division

Industrialization

Women

Liberty

Love and Love

Affairs

South and North

Set 3		Set 4	

Seoul

Tradition

Avant-Garde

Diaspora

Family

Humor

Search "bilingual edition

can meet the real Korea!
Korean Literature

22 keywords to understand Korean literature

korean literature"on Amazon!